Chuckles

Written by Helene Greenstein
Illustrated by Barbara Zagha

Dedicated to our grandchildren

Chuckles was a small gray Bunny. He had smooth fur on his chest and body. He liked to take a snooze every hour.

But Chuckles was very special.
He was born with particularly large, floppy feet.

Chuckles had siblings named Bruce and Thumper. They were born in a swampy thicket deep in the forest where birds chirped cheerily, bees buzzed and winds whistled.

Mommy bunny fed Chuckles, Bruce and Thumper until they were big enough to forage for their own food.

One day they snuck down to the creek, sniffing for chicory and choke berries.

The rocks created shaggy shapes,
sometimes looking like sharks or snakes.

The scared bunnies quickly and quietly hopped away so as not to disturb the fearsome creatures. They scurried off in search of chunky cherries.

One morning Chuckles spotted a splendid shimmering bunny with velvety white fur. The fluffy bunny smelled so sweet and had cheeks that stuck out like marshmallows. Even his chin was cheerfully charming.

Chuckles thought this strange new visitor was the most glorious creature he had ever encountered.

The shimmering, lovely, bunny was on his way to find the snowy paradise he called home. Chuckles asked, “Can I come?” The plucky bunny “*Tsk-tsked*” and answered that Chuckles was too small to leave his mommy.

Chuckles was sad. He longed to be like the brave Bunny.

Chuckles was determined to find the fine looking bunny. He chomped on strings of strawberries. He gnawed twigs of bark and blades of leafy weeds so he could grow big and strong.

Finally, Chuckles was ready. He packed his small bag, kissed his family goodbye and set off on his adventure.

After quite a while of hopping he heard chattering. Out jumped three bunnies from behind tall stalks. "*Hello*" they all shrieked together.

Chuckles was surprised and shouted, "*Hello, who are you*?" "We are three sisters, Frickles, Vickles and Pickles."

" We do everything together. We sleep and creep and flop and plop together. We greet and eat and have big feet together. Would you like to come with us?"

"Thank you very much," replied Chuckles,
"I am on my way to find a bunny the color of snow ."

"Oh well, have a nice trip," chimed the three sisters as they bounded away.

Chuckles continued on his journey. He was getting hungry and tired, so he stopped to snack on droopy carrots and limp celery sticks packed earlier in his satchel.

Then he threw down his blanket of straw, closed his weary eyes and fell asleep.

When Chuckles awoke, he grabbed his valise
and continued on his way. He found himself at a train depot.

A boxcar door was open and Chuckles hopped inside.
He found a warm dark corner where he settled down to rest.

As the train started to roll along the tracks, he fell fast asleep to the gentle rocking and the clickety-clack of the wheels on the tracks.

Hours later, Chuckles awakened to find the train had stopped rolling. The door was open and Chuckles peeked outside at a wonderland of snow. The air was cold and his breath puffed out a stream of smoke.

Chuckles scampered to the ground and looked high above the station to see a mountain covered in soft fluffy clouds that looked like bunnies. He had arrived at the place where the splendid bunny lived.

Chuckles grasped his bag and set out towards the mountain.
He skipped and bounced until he was at the highest point.

He discovered a thicket of branches and found many bunnies but none was the bunny with the fluffiest fur and cheeks as big as marshmallows.

He asked the bunnies, "Do you know where the most beautiful brave bunny with the fluffiest fur lives?" None of the bunnies answered.

Chuckles was tired so he bedded down in the snow, and dreamed of his mother and brothers. He slept for many hours. It was cold in the snow, but he slept on.

The next morning when Chuckles awoke all the bunnies were staring at him with surprise. Chuckles swept the sleep from his eyes and shook himself off.

Again he asked, “Do you know where the most beautiful bunny lives?”

All the bunnies pointed to the nearby lake. Chuckles crept forward to the frozen pond and looked down into the cold water. Reflected in the ice was the most beautiful white bunny he had ever seen.

He drew closer and blinked his eyes. The frozen bunny blinked his eye Chuckles wrinkled his pink nose. The bunny wrinkled his nose. During the cold night Chuckles fur had turned white.

Chuckles frolicked with the Snow White bunnies all through the day. He came to a hill and rolled happily down the side of the mountain.

He passed big boulders and trees that had new leaves. The grass grew green and high. Soon he was far away from the other bunnies.

He began to feel the sunshine making him warm. He found himself at a sparkling pond and bent down to take a drink. Staring back at him was a beautiful gray bunny.

Chuckles wrinkled his nose.
The gray bunny wrinkled his nose.
Chuckles blinked his eyes.
The gray bunny blinked his eyes.
Chuckles had found a beautiful gray bunny.
Chuckles had found himself.
He was beautiful in every color.
The beautiful bunny was always HIM.

The End

About the Authors

Helene Greenstein

Helene has been storytelling from a young age, drawing from her love of fables, fairytales and fantasies. She strives to teach youngsters kindness, courage and strength to overcome challenges using humorous stories and characters.

The story was conceived as a way to aid children with speech challenges. This is her first publication where she has incorporated many combination sounds which can be challenging to new young readers. She has goals to write more stories concentrating on other challenging sounds and letters.

Barbara Zagha

Barbara Zagha's artistic vision is a celebration of life, drawing from a wealth of personal, professional and spiritual influences. Her artistic voice is expressed in multiple media including watercolors, pastels, photography, pencil, pen & ink and oil. Watercolors are her primary focus and most reflective of her signature style. Her colleagues of mixed media are now part of her book illustrating. Barbara is often inspired and ceaslessly supported by her loving family.

Made in the USA
Middletown, DE
14 October 2023

40243223R00018